Table of Contents

Rourke™

Can you find these words?

craters

desert

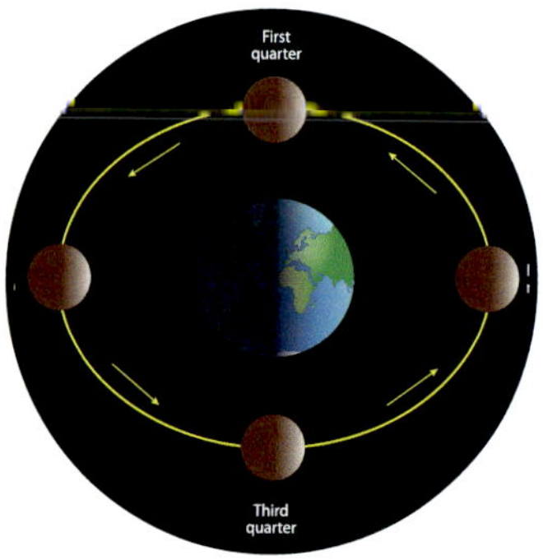

orbits

tides

Our Moon

The moon is our nearest neighbor.

It **orbits** around Earth.
It takes a month to go around once.

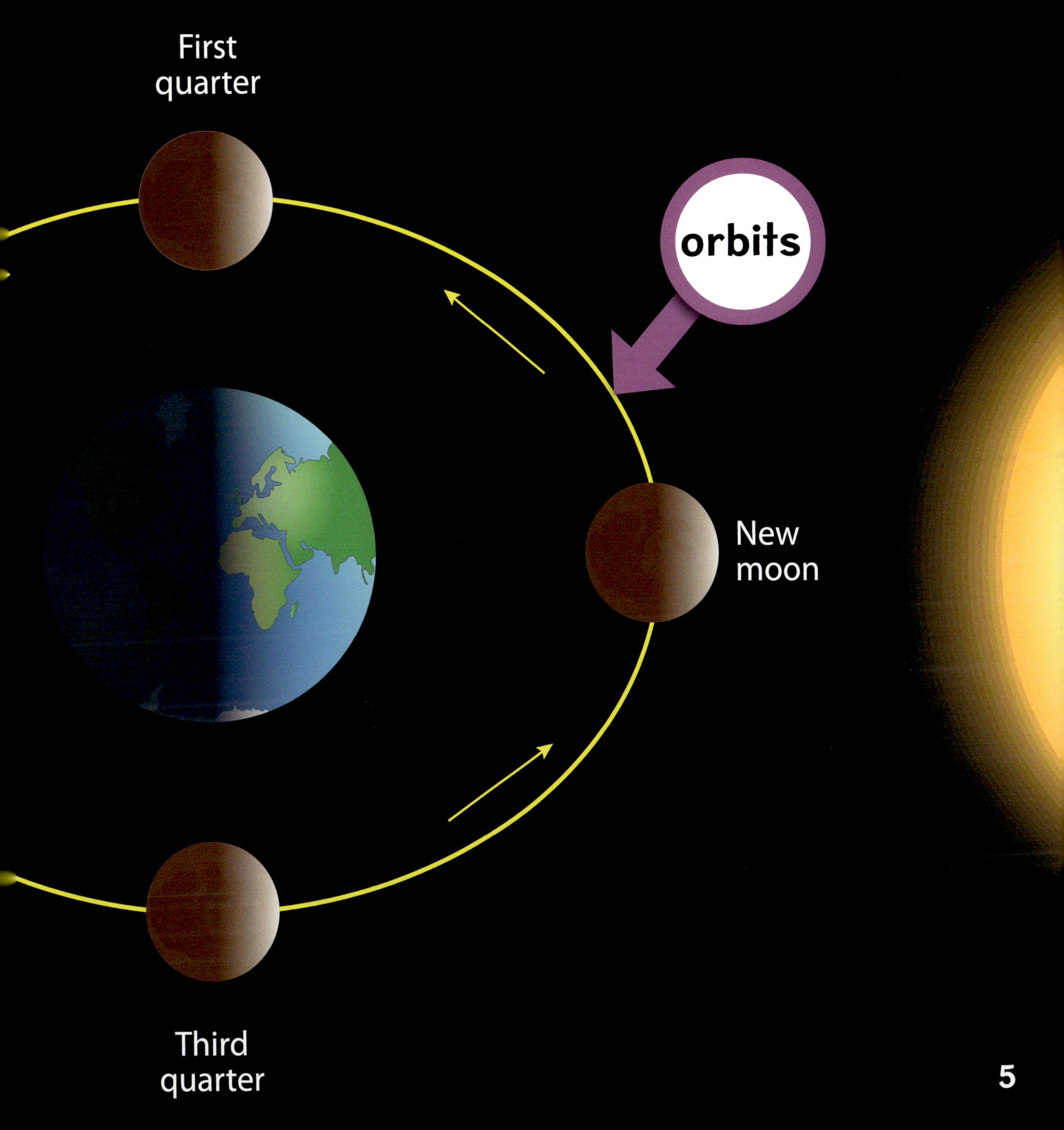
First quarter
orbits
New moon
Third quarter

Our moon pulls on Earth.

It makes **tides** go up.
It makes tides go down.

Our moon is dry.

It is drier than a **desert**.

But there is water on our moon.

Our moon has **craters**.
There is water in the craters.

Our moon is like a mirror.

It reflects the sun's light.

Did you find these words?

Our moon has **craters.**

It is drier than a **desert.**

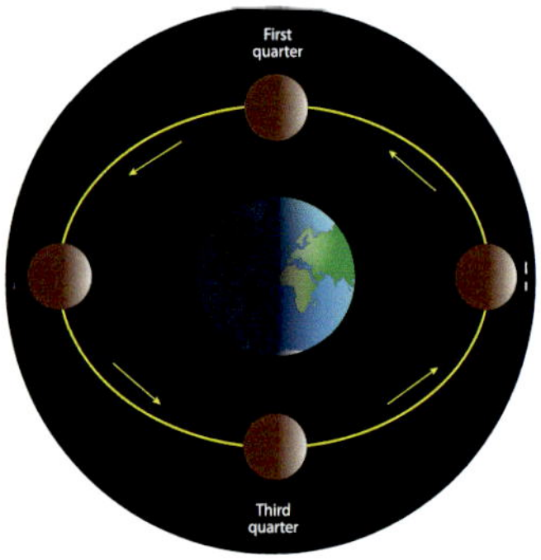

It **orbits** around Earth.

It makes **tides** go up.

Photo Glossary

craters (KRAY-turs): Large holes in the ground.

desert (DEZ-urt): A dry area with little or no rain where few plants grow.

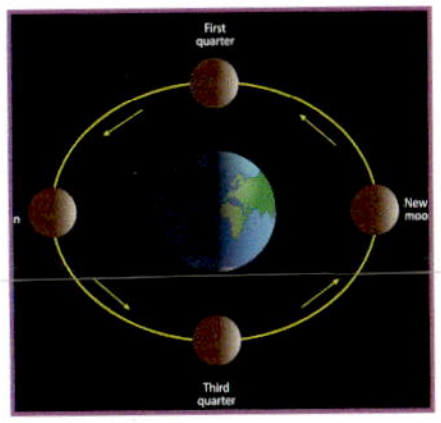

orbits (OR-bits): Travels in a circular path around something.

tides (tides): The constant changes in sea level caused by the pull of the sun and the moon.

Index

About the Author

Lori Mortensen lives in Northern California with her family and her cat, Max. When she's not tapping away at her computer, she likes to go on long walks just before sunrise and see the sun and moon together in the morning sky.

www.rourkebooks.com

PHOTO CREDITS: Cover: 4FR; p. 2,10,14,15: ©ALEXEY FILATOV; p. 2,9,14,15: ©Fabio Lamanna; p. 2,6,14,15: ©J'nel; p. 3: ©pjmorley; p. 8: ©HelenField; p. 12: ©foto-ruhrgebiet

Edited by: Keli Sipperley
Cover and interior design by: Rhea Magaro-Wallace

Library of Congress PCN Data
Our Moon / Lori Mortensen
(Discovery Days)
ISBN (hard cover)(alk. paper) 978-1-64156-176-1
ISBN (soft cover) 978-1-64156-232-4
ISBN (e-Book) 978-1-64156-284-3
Library of Congress Control Number: 2017957785

Printed in the United States of America
01-2832211937